Empathy

by Jayneen Sanders
illustrated by Cherie Zamazing

Using Little BIG Chats

The *Little BIG Chats* series has been written to assist parents, caregivers and educators to have open and age-appropriate conversations with young children around crucial, and yet at times, 'tough' topics. And what better way than using children's picture books! Some pages will have questions for your child to interact with and discuss. Feel free to use these questions and the Discussion Questions provided on the inside back cover of this book to help you assist your child with the topic being explored. Stop at any time to unpack the text together; and try to follow your child's lead wherever that conversation may take you! So, please, get comfy and start some empowering 'chats' around some BIG topics with your child.

The Body Safety titles should ideally be read in the following order: *Consent*, *My Safety Network*, *My Early Warning Signs*, *Private Parts are Private*, and *Secrets and Surprises*. The remaining titles can be read in any order.

Hi! I'm Asha.
Today we're learning
about empathy
and kindness.

Empathy is a very
important word.

It means you
understand what
someone else is feeling.

It means you are
kind and caring.

If someone is sad
because they fell over —
being kind and caring
is important.

You could ask the person
if they are okay.

You could say,
'I'm so sorry you
fell over. It must have
really hurt. Can I help?'

If someone feels shy because they are new at your school — being kind and caring is important.

You could show the new person around and play with them at lunch time.

You could say, 'I know how you feel. I felt shy when I first came to this school. Would you like to play with me?'

If a big person you know well looks really busy — being kind and caring is important.

You could offer to help them.

You could say, 'You look really busy. That must be hard for you. Can I help?'

If a person is scared
because the slide looks
too scary for them
to come down —
being kind and caring
is important.

You could cheer them on.

You could say,
'You are brave.
I think you can do this!'

Showing other people you care about them and you understand their feelings makes you feel happy inside too.

Empathy makes the world a much nicer place.

Every day we are learning.
And we can learn empathy
from each other!